BE KIND; EVERYONE Y ... A HARD
BATTLE.

–JOHN WATSON

THE NEW KID

Maureen Straka

CONTENTS

CHAPTER 1

Goodbye Luke

Having your best friend move away is like finding a week-old tuna sandwich in the bottom of your back pack. It really stinks. When Luke moved away last summer, I knew things wouldn't be the same. Luke was more than just my best friend. He was the coolest person I've ever known.

He could beat every level on Space Pod Invasion.

He could burp the entire alphabet, forwards... *and backwards*.

He could blast a baseball clear over the fence at Parker Field.

In gym class, he was *always* chosen team captain. And for some reason, he always picked me first, even though I was the shortest kid in class.

I still remember that day last August when he broke the news. That afternoon was so hot, I thought the rubber might melt right off my high tops. Dad was grilling burgers, while we were splashing around in the pool with my kid brother Dylan, trying to knock him off his dinosaur raft. My mom yelled at us to leave him alone, so we hopped out to shoot some hoops.

We played for about 5 minutes and Luke was winning (no surprise), but I wasn't that far behind. The score was 7 to 9, and just as Mom called us for dinner, I managed to sink a three- pointer from the corner of the driveway which pulled me into the lead 10-9.

"Oh yeah! Feel the burn because Alex Baker is on fire," I shouted. "Ladies and Gentleman, I do believe that history has been made tonight," I said into an imaginary microphone. "Alex Baker beat Luke 'Hoops' McKinley. He is the new reigning champion of Butler Avenue. The crowd is going wild! Raaaaaaah!"

Luke smiled and wiped the sweat from his forehead. "Pure luck, Dude. Besides you were bound to win one before I left town."

"Hey, it's not that bad. You don't have to pack your bags just because you lost," I laughed.

"Actually, I do," he said.

Suddenly, Luke had a weird look on his face.

"What do you mean?" I asked.

He took a deep breath and wiped his nose with the back of his hand. "You know how my parents don't get along." He dribbled the ball and sunk a long shot.

"Yeah, I know. You can sleep over again tonight if you want. My parents don't mind."

I knew his parents fought a lot. Sometimes I could hear them through my open window at night. It was really bad when I heard doors slamming or dishes breaking. On those nights, Luke would show up at our door. I didn't ask any questions, just dug out a sleeping bag and an extra pillow from the closet.

"Yeah, I know," he said. "That's what makes this so hard." He swallowed and looked down. "My parents are getting a divorce," he said, kicking the pavement.

"Oh, wow. That's tough. Sorry, Man."

"That's not the worst part," Luke said. By the way he was biting his lip, it looked like he was trying not to cry. That scared me. I only saw Luke cry once before when his dog, Ranger, was hit by a car. I knew he was really upset.

"My mom is moving to New York… and she's taking me with her."

I felt like I'd been punched in the stomach. We stood there for a while, silent. Then Luke shook his head. "You don't realize how lucky you are, Dude. You've got things so easy."

I wasn't sure what he meant. He had everything over me. He was at least 10 inches taller than me, great at sports, and everyone liked him, even Emily, the prettiest girl in school.

I shook my head and sighed. "Sorry, Dude."

Just one week later, I stood in Luke's driveway and watched his moving truck drive away. My stomach twisted like a pretzel, as I thought about starting middle school on my own.

CHAPTER 2

Sand Castles in the Kitchen

The rest of the summer could be summed up with one word. BORING!

All I had done since Luke left was watch *Captain Destruction* cartoons and play Alien Invaders on X-Games. I made it to level 17, which was amazing since I survived attacks from the most dangerous brain-sucking zombie aliens, but my parents didn't appreciate this accomplishment.

Whenever my dad walked by my room, he shook his head and grumbled. My mom was a little more sympathetic, but after a week of Alien Invaders, she pulled the plug.

I was minutes away from level 18, when she stormed in my room, armed with a basket full of laundry and just yanked the plug from the wall. I gasped, as the TV screen faded to black. Socks spilled from the laundry basket like fallen alien zombies.

"Oh my gosh, Mom. Why did you do that?" I didn't save my game. Now I'll have to start all over at the beginning of level 17."

Mom rolled her eyes and scooped up the socks, tossing them back into the basket. "Alex, I've had it with you moping around this house. It's been 5 days since Luke left, and you've been glued to that video game ever since. I'm very sorry that your best friend moved away. We all miss him. But life goes on. And the best way to get over it is by keeping busy. So, put your laundry away and clean up this room." She pointed to the empty chip bags on my dresser and dirty socks on the floor.

My room *was* starting to smell like a combination of nacho chips and feet.

"Then go outside and get some sunshine. Why don't you go over to Danielle's house? Maybe you can ride bikes for a bit."

I groaned. "Danielle is a major pain in the butt."

"Alex, that's no way to talk about your cousin." Mom stuffed some T-shirts in my top drawer, and dropped the basket on my bed, motioning for me to put the rest of the clothes away.

"Mom, you know how she is. She always tries to boss me around."

The only good thing about living across the street from Danielle is that she's best friends with Emily.

Emily with the blue eyes and killer smile.

Emily who made my knees feel like Jell-O.

Emily who'd spent a lot of time smiling at Luke.

Before Luke left, sometimes we'd ride our bikes with Danielle and Emily along Dead Man's Curve. The girls would get real nervous because it's a narrow path that wraps around the river. We tried to act brave, but it made us nervous, too.

I sighed. "Alright, I'll go over her house, but only for a little while."

"Great, because when you get back I need you to watch Dylan. I'm giving Mrs. Rader a perm today."

My mom had a beauty salon in the front room of our house and Mrs. Rader was one of her oldest customers. She had a little toy poodle named Peanut. She brought Peanut in her purse everywhere she went, even to the beauty shop. Dylan loved the dog, but he thought she was a stuffed animal. The first time he saw

Peanut, he squealed, "Puppy!", and tried to pick her up by her tail. I rescued poor Peanut before the monster could hurt her, but Mrs. Rader turned so red I thought her head would explode. Since then, Mom put a restraining order on Dylan whenever Peanut is nearby.

I finished up my room, took a deep breath, and then headed back outside into the real world. There were only three days left of summer vacation, and I figured I should try to make the most of them. Shielding my eyes in the bright sun, I trudged across the street to Danielle's house, hoping maybe Emily would be there. I swatted at a mosquito buzzing near my ear and rang the doorbell, waiting for the boss of the world to grace me with her presence. Danielle appeared in the door with her hands on her hips, snapping her gum in the annoying way she always does.

"Well, well, well…. Look who crawled out of his cave." She eyed me carefully, raising an eyebrow. "Are you sure you can survive out here in the wild without Luke?"

"Shut up, Danielle," I said, peering over her shoulder to see if she had company. I frowned. No sign of Emily.

"You want to ride bikes, or what?" I mumbled.

She sighed dramatically, "Yeah, I guess so. Who else is going to watch after my little cousin?" Danielle was only two and a half months older than me, but she was about six inches taller, and she seemed to think that made her much older. She drove me CRAZY!

I gritted my teeth and hopped on my bike, pumping hard down the pebble path leading to Deadman's Curve. The rock crunched beneath my tires, as Danielle tried to catch up.

"Alex, not so fast! Don't ride so close to the edge- you want to fall in the river?" She was worse than my mom. I was actually looking forward to babysitting, just so I could get away from her.

After one loop around Deadman's curve, I'd had enough. I shouted, "See ya," and left Danielle in the dust. I pretended not to hear her shouting, "Slow down!", as I raced home. I shoved my bike in our shed and headed inside.

Mrs. Rader was already sitting in the beauty shop, clutching Peanut as if she was protecting him from an evil monster. Dylan was crawling on the floor pushing his toy train around her ankles. She shook her head and kicked her feet away from Dylan, huddling Peanut closer.

I smiled, trying not to laugh. "Oh hi, Mrs. Rader."

She snorted in return, turning a brighter shade of red.

"Alex, please keep an eye on him," Mom said, shooting me a look.

"Okay. Let's go Buddy," I said, pushing his train with my foot towards the living room. Dylan followed along, crawling after his train.

I grabbed a bag of popcorn from the kitchen and flopped on the living room couch to watch *Captain Destruction*. Dylan was in the corner of the room playing with at his train table. *That should keep him busy for a while*, I thought. The kid really loved his trains. He had a name for each one and could play with them for hours. I didn't realize he was gone until the commercial break. That's when I heard him laughing in the kitchen.

Oh no. This can't be good, I thought.

I found him sitting in the middle of the kitchen floor dumping iced tea mix everywhere. I saw three empty cans turned over behind him, and a huge mound of brown powder in the middle of the tile. I honestly think my heart stopped.

"Dylan, what the heck are you doing?" I asked, as I glanced at the door to make sure that mom was still in the shop. He looked up at me with these big puppy eyes and said, "Alex, I'm making sand castles, want to play?"

"Sandcastles!" I stammered. "If Mom sees this mess, we'll be lucky if we live to ever see the beach again." I grabbed a bucket from the closet and tried to wash up the mess. There was just one problem.

Water + Iced Tea Mix = ICED TEA

Now instead of powder, there was a thick brown puddle of sticky iced tea goo in the middle of the kitchen floor. The more I tried to clean it, the more tea I made.

Then I heard footsteps and knew I was a goner. The door opened and I swear my mom's jaw almost hit the floor. She took one look at the brown swamp and dropped her perm rods. I didn't know what else to do, so I smiled and said, "Hey Mom, want some iced tea?"

She didn't think that was very funny and *I* ended up getting sent to my room. Did Dylan get in trouble? NO. Totally unfair. But that's the way things go around here.

I spent the rest of the day alone in my room, which is kind of like being trapped in preschool. I have to share my room with the little monster which is majorly uncool. No self-respecting twelve-year old should have stuffed animals on his dresser and posters of a purple dinosaur hanging on his walls. I tried to explain this to my parents, but they told me I should be grateful to have a roof over my head.

I'd come to realize 3 things about my parents:

1. You just can't reason with them.

2. They have no idea what it's like being 12.

3. They blame me for anything that Dylan does.

I tried to make the most of my jail time. I practiced shooting my dart gun at Dylan's stuffed dinosaur. Why would they make a dinosaur purple? It's not even realistic. So, I have to admit it was kind of fun ambushing him, but that goofy dinosaur just sat there on the dresser smiling at me.

When I got bored, I sang karaoke on my new machine that I got for my birthday, but you can only sing *Born to Be Wild* so many times before you go hoarse. And without Luke playing air guitar it wasn't very fun. That's when I heard a truck pull up next door. I wondered if it was my new neighbors.

I pulled the curtain back and I saw this kid walking towards Luke's house carrying a glass tank with some kind of weird lizard animal inside. He had thick glasses and his hair stuck up in the back. He was wearing dark jeans and weird looking saddle shoes. I sighed and closed the curtain. He was nothing like Luke. But I told myself, school would be starting next week and there'd be other kids to hang out with. The question was without Luke around, would they still want to hang out with me?

CHAPTER 3

A Bad Start

I overslept on the first day of school. Yeah, yeah, yeah, I know what you're thinking. How could anyone oversleep on their first day? So irresponsible, blah..blah..blah.... Believe me I heard it all from my parents that morning, but it really wasn't my fault. I barely got any sleep the night before. And it wasn't like I stayed up late playing video games or watching TV. It was because of Dylan. He was on a monster-in-the-closet kick, and I was at his mercy.

He woke up screaming at least ten times during the night. I tried everything to get him to go back to sleep, but nothing worked.

I put on the hall light. No luck.

I dug an old flashlight out of our toy box and let him hold it, but he shined it in my eyes like every three minutes asking, "Alex, are you awake? Did you hear that noise? I think the monster just sneezed."

Finally, he ended up crawling in my bed, sleeping with his feet in my face.

So, when that alarm clock started beeping at seven o'clock, I thought it was part of my dream. I was dreaming that an ice cream truck was driving down my street with it's bells ringing. I was chasing after it waving my two dollars, trying to catch up to it. When I took a closer look, I saw that it was Luke driving the truck, waving as the truck disappeared down the street. That's when Dylan rolled over and kicked me in the face, finally waking me up.

"Oh God! It's 7:45. No time to shower! I'll miss the bus." I shouted.

I jumped into my new jeans, tripping over my feet. Then I dug a green polo shirt, from my hamper and gave it a quick sniff. It would have to do. I squirted a blob of gel in my hand and pulled it through my hair. I was going for that "messy look", but it looked a little more like bed head.

I hurried to the kitchen to scarf down some Captain Cocoa because the bus would be there any minute. Dylan was busy playing under the table. I pulled out a chair and sat down. That's when I felt the squish.

"What the heck?" I jumped up and felt the gooey mess on the back of my pants. I looked down at the chair and saw a paint brush lying in a puddle of brown paint.

"O, God. It's paint!" I glared at my mom and said, "He left his paintbrush on the chair. My pants are a mess and the bus will be here any second. You've got to do something!"

Dylan popped his head out from under the table and said, "Alex, did you go poopy in your pants? You should use the potty." I was about to let him have it when I heard the screech of the bus's brakes outside.

"Oh God, Mom. Help!" Mom grabbed some paper towels and tried rubbing the brown stain off the back of my pants. She got most of it out, but now I had a big wet spot in the back.

"Go ahead Alex, you're fine. It will be dry by the time you get to school."

I didn't have a choice. I grabbed my lunch and rushed out the door.

There were only two empty seats left on the bus, one next to Danielle and one next to the new kid. He was wearing those dark jeans and the goofy saddle shoes. He looked up and smiled a big hope-we-can-be-friends grin, and then he dropped his pencil case. A sea of colored pencils rolled across the floor. I knew that I should help him pick them up, but I stepped over them and kept walking. It was going to be hard enough starting middle school without Luke, but sitting with this kid could be the kiss of death. He just seemed too weird. I had to fend for myself. So, I sat next to Danielle, but right away I knew that was a big mistake.

Danielle giggled. "Alex, what's wrong with your pants. You have a big wet spot on them. Honestly, Alex, you should try to make yourself look more presentable. After all, it is the first day of middle school."

I shrugged. "Gee, thanks for the advice. You look nice, too."

She rattled on about school for the entire ride. I lost interest when she started blabbing about our new teacher Ms. Riley, saying she looked like a hippie. I tried staring out the window and tuning her out. Not a great start for my first day. Things had to get better from here, right?

CHAPTER 4

The First Day

I stepped off the bus and took a deep breath. I looked at the large building looming ahead and I suddenly felt very small. Sure, we drove past Kennedy Middle School all the time, but when you're walking up those concrete steps and through the big wooden doors, it suddenly seems a whole lot bigger. *You can do this*, I told myself.

I stumbled through the stream of students and looked around. It was nothing like my elementary school, which was always decorated with welcome back signs, and apples, and happy faces. This place looked more like a factory. There were long hallways lined with an endless stream of lockers. Each time I turned a corner, there was yet another corridor crammed with students. Most of them looked a heck of a lot older than me. I felt like a rat scurrying through a maze to find a chunk of cheese. In this case, the cheese was room 6B.

Somehow, I found my classroom. Ms. Riley was standing at the door waiting for us. She was wearing a long flowery skirt and a crazy looking grin. She made a big fuss over each student as they passed through the door.

"Well, hello there. What's your name?" she asked me.

"Uhh..Alex Baker."

Suddenly it felt like the first day of kindergarten.

"Well, Alex. Welcome to sixth grade. I'm Ms. Riley, but you can call me Judy. You go ahead in and find your seat. There's a little surprise waiting for you at your desk."

"Okay," I mumbled.

Entering the room, I felt like I was on a jungle safari. There were leafy plants everywhere, covering the windowsills, tables, and bookcase. And there were tons of class pets. I don't mean pets like Danielle, who knows the answer to every question a teacher asks before she even asks it. I mean real pets, like hamsters, frogs, and goldfish. Their tanks lined the tables at the back of the room. This probably explains why it smelled a little like a zoo.

Ms. Riley had a nameplate on each desk. I found mine at the front of the room next to the new kid. He just kept popping up everywhere. He was sitting there arranging those colored pencils in his pencil box. Geez, he sure had a thing for art supplies. I glanced at his nameplate and saw Simon spelled with a big swirly 'S'.

I sat down and found a happy face lollipop on my desk. It said *SMILE.* I rolled my eyes. I certainly didn't feel like there was much to smile about.

I saw Emily was sitting two rows over and gulped. I hoped that brown stain was gone off my pants. I shifted in my seat trying to hide the spot, just in case. TJ Hinkleman was on my other side. He could be a real jerk, but Luke always knew how to put him in his place.

He looked over and said, "Hey Baker, what's goin' on?"

"Not much, TJ. How was your summer?"

"One word to describe it...EPIC. You are looking at the starting quarterback for the Bulldogs and so far we are undefeated," he said, smiling. "Thanks to me."

TJ was wearing his brother's Leroy's #14 football jersey. Leroy had been a star quarterback his senior year. It was TJ's claim to fame.

"Hey where's your buddy, Luke?" he asked.

I looked down at my notebook and bit my lip. "He uhh…moved to New York."

T.J grinned. "Oh, really."

"But, he'll be back to visit soon," I added quickly, hoping it was true.

He nodded to the new kid and said, "What's with this new dude? Check out those glasses. They're thicker than my Grandma's."

He leaned over and yelled, "Hey kid, did anyone ever tell you those glasses make you look like a bug?"

Simon looked up, his eyes wide behind his thick frames. He laughed a little, but his face kind of fell.

"And what's with the shoes? Did you do your school shopping at a yard sale? Dude, you are having a serious wardrobe malfunction."

Simon was turning a little red now, but still trying to smile. He said in a quiet voice, "The shoes…" He paused for a moment. "They're hand-me-downs."

"More like hand-me-don'ts," TJ snickered.

His friend Randy joined in, "Hand-me-don'ts. That's a good one, Dude."

Simon stared down at his pencil box.

"And what's with the colored pencils? Do you think this is Kindergarten?" TJ just wouldn't let up. "Oooh, I forgot my crayons!" He turned to me, smirking. "Baker, Can I borrow your glue stick? I want to make a craft for mommy."

I laughed, but then I looked over at Simon. By now his face was so red that it looked like his ears were ready to catch fire. I felt kind of bad for him. It had to be hard being in a brand-new school and not knowing anyone. Luke would have told TJ to shut up and give the kid a break, but I just sat there. I was afraid that if I opened my mouth, I might be TJ's next victim.

Then Simon started sniffing and pulled a crumpled old tissue out of his shirt sleeve. He started wiping his nose. *Oh, God. It's like he's asking for it,* I thought.

When TJ saw the tissue, his jaw dropped. "You've got to be kidding me, Dude. Tissues in your sleeve? What's your problem?"

Simon opened his mouth to answer, but then his face kind of scrunched up. He huffed and heaved and then the sneezing began. I swear he must have sneezed at least twenty times. I thought the kid was taking a seizure.

Ms. Riley came rushing over and asked, "Are you alright, Simon?"

Simon sniffed and said, "I'm okay. It's just my allergies. I'm allergic to chalk dust,"

Then TJ pretended to sneeze and said, "I'm allergic to dorks."

Randy burst out laughing, but Ms. Riley spun around and stared at TJ, not even a hint of that silly grin on her face. "Rule number one: We do not insult one another in room 6B. This is not a place for negative energy."

TJ snickered. I had a feeling he had plenty more negative energy to share. Ms. Riley went on about karma for about ten minutes. By that time, TJ lost interest and was busy bending paper clips into little boomerangs. I wondered who he was planning to use them on.

During lunch, I steered clear of TJ and sat by Danielle. Sure, I had to listen to her ramble on about her favorite band *No Direction*, but it was better than hanging out with TJ and Randy.

Simon was sitting by himself at the front of the cafeteria. I thought about asking him if he wanted to sit with us. I knew Luke would have done that. But I was already stressed out enough.

I was glad when the day was over. My plan was to keep my mouth shut, cause no trouble, and just survive 6th grade. Too bad things don't always go as well as planned.

CHAPTER 5

More Changes

When I got home from school that day, Dad was already there. It was weird because he usually worked until supper time. He was sitting in the Lazy Boy looking at TV, but not really watching, just kind of staring into space.

I cleared my throat. "Hi, Dad." I didn't think he heard me at first. "Hey Dad, why are you home so early? You feeling okay?"

He looked up startled. "Oh hi, Alex. I'm fine. I uhh…I just had a tough day at work." He shook his head and sighed. "I guess you'll be seeing me around the house a bit more." He smiled, but his eyes looked sad. Something wasn't right.

"That's good, right?" I giggled, a stupid habit of mine. I always laugh when I'm scared.

Dad shrugged. "Well, I'm glad to be home with you, but the circumstances aren't the best, Son. You see, my company has been having a rough year, making a lot of cut backs. And well… they had to let me go."

The words echoed in my ear for a moment before I figured out what he meant.

Let him go? As in fired?

My Dad had been selling insurance for Keller & Smith forever. Dad took me to work with him on take-your-kid-to-work-day. I sat in his chair and spun around until I was ready to toss my cookies.

We had his boss, Mr. Smith, over for dinner and he had *two* servings of Mom's lasagna. Two servings. Which meant no leftovers for my lunch! And just last month, I raced in the three-legged race at the company picnic with Mr. Smith. We would have won, too, if it weren't for the freak accident.

It was just awful. We were in the lead, only five feet from the finish line, and I thought for sure we'd win. But then this huge crow swooped down from a tree. I think he was after a burnt hotdog that Dylan left on the picnic table. I heard a caw and I looked up. That's when I felt the splat! I reached up and felt the sticky glob on my neck.

"Ewwwwww…. Gross! He pooped on me!" I yelled. I lost my balance and fell forward. I tumbled and pulled Mr. Smith down with me, twisting his ankle. Dylan and Dad won the race. Dad hoisted Dylan on his shoulder, waving the trophy in the air. He was oblivious to me and Mr. Smith, the tangled three-legged heap nearby. Me, splattered with crow poop. And poor Mr. Smith… he ended up on crutches.

Suddenly it dawned on me.

His ankle! They fired Dad because I hurt Mr. Smith's ankle!

I looked at Dad and didn't know what to say. I cleared my throat. "Well uhh.., I better go start my homework." I rambled. "I have a ton of Math. Long division, you know how LONG that can take, right?"

Dad didn't get my corny joke. He was back to staring at the infomercial, so I made a quick escape to my room.

I couldn't believe that they fired Dad all because of me. I cranked up my stereo and tried to work on my homework, but it was hard to concentrate. I kept thinking about Dad and the sad look on his face. He looked the way I did when I brought home a bad report card. Later that night, I burrowed under my covers. I could hear Dylan snoring softly and my parents talking through my closed door. They were trying to be quiet, but I could make out certain words.

"Laid-off... mortgage payments....lose the house."

Holy crud. As if things weren't bad enough, now we might lose our house, too? And it was all my fault.

I covered my head with my pillow, blocking out my parents' serious voices. But I couldn't get rid of the awful sinking feeling in my stomach.

That night I dreamed that a giant bird pooped on our house and gobbled me up whole. Then he spit me back out with a broken ankle. And TJ Hinkleman came along, stole my crutches, and stuffed me in a locker.

I woke up in a cold sweat, determined to fix this situation. Before I left for school, I sat at my desk and wrote Mr. Smith a letter.

Dear Mr. Smith,

I am soooo sorry for hurting your ankle at the company picnic. I had no idea what that crazy bird would do. If only he had been flying in a different direction or maybe laid off the berries, we could have avoided the whole situation. Anyway, please don't blame my Dad. If you need to blame someone, blame me, or the bird, or the bird's bad aim. And please hire my Dad back. It really wasn't his fault. I could send you money from my allowance each week to cover your doctor's bills. It's not much, but it might help.

Sincerely,

Alex Baker, proud sharer of Mom's lasagna (2 helpings)

It couldn't hurt to work the lasagna angle. Desperate times call for desperate measures. I stuffed the letter in my back pack and decided to deliver it to Dad's office right after school.

CHAPTER 6

The Great Fish Catastrophe

Dad's office was only a few blocks from school and I figured I could skip the bus and walk home instead, sliding the letter under his office door. However, my plan had a minor glitch. And that glitch had fins and blew bubbles.

You see, Mrs. Riley had this goldfish named Emeril. (I think she named him after the guy on the cooking show.) Anyway, she kept it in a glass bowl in the back of the room. She decided to have each student in our class take the goldfish home for a night. She got a notebook and she wrote *Emeril's Travels* on the cover. We were supposed to take it home and make a journal entry of all of the things that the fish saw while he spent the night at each of our houses. It would probably be a neat idea for 1st graders, but not so neat when you're in 6th grade.

Ms. Riley seemed really excited about the assignment. You could tell she thought it was real a winner. She had this big smile and she kept moving her hands around in the air while she was talking.

She looked at the roll book and said, "Let's see who will be our first fish foster parent."

Lucky me, I was at the top of the class list. She called out my name and flashed that crazy smile. I sighed and headed to the front of the room. I saw her smile fade a little when I rolled my eyes, so I pretended I was just looking up at the ceiling. She proudly held out her prized possession along with a jar of fish flakes.

"Just a pinch or two is all he needs." Then she looked at me and smiled. "I know you'll take good care of him, Alex."

"Sure, Ms. Riley," I said, my cheeks burning.

I placed the fishbowl on the corner of my desk and wondered how the heck I would get it home. It would be a long walk home carrying my book bag and a fishbowl. And after the whole tripping incident during the 3-legged race, I didn't trust myself getting Emeril home safely. I had visions of taking a face plant on Main Street, water spilling and poor Emeril flopping around on the sidewalk. So, I figured my best bet was to take the bus. But the bus ride was tough because our bus driver, "Speedy" Springer was not what you would call a cautious driver.

Somehow, I got the fish home without getting totally soaked and I put the bowl on my dresser. I had a lot on my mind. I had to figure how to get the letter to Mr. Smith and write a dumb fish diary. I forgot about Emeril until after supper, when I was sitting at the kitchen table trying to write the stupid fish journal.

Dylan sat on the floor playing with his toy cars and it was really hard to concentrate because he kept making these "Vroom-vroom" noises.

I sighed. "Mom, can't he do that in the other room?"

"He's not bothering anyone, just start your work," she replied.

I sighed. "Okay. I'm the fish. What did I do during my exciting stay at Alex's house?"

I picked up my pencil and wrote *I swam around the bowl all day blowing bubbles and looking at Alex's room.* I read it out loud and it sounded kind of dumb.

"What else can I say about the fish?" I asked.

Mom was standing at the sink rinsing the dishes. "Why don't you say what the fish saw, from his point of view in the tank," she suggested.

I closed my eyes and pictured my bedroom.

"Okay here goes." I pretended to read aloud from the journal. "It's not very neat in here. There are smelly socks on the floor and a Doritos bag on the dresser. I think this room would look much better with a flat screen TV, instead of the dumb dinosaur posters."

"Nice try." Mom smiled. "Maybe you could talk about the bus ride home."

Suddenly Dylan sat up and shouted, "I know, Alex. Tell about the fishy's bath."

At first, I didn't pay attention, I thought he was just babbling about the fish. Then he said, "The fishy took a bubble bath. He wanted to get clean."

I looked at him and asked really slowly, "Who gave the fish a bubble bath?"

He had this big proud grin on his face. "I did. With lots of bubbles. It made fishy tired and now he's sleeping."

I knew that didn't sound good. I raced upstairs to the bathroom. I checked the tub and breathed a sigh of relief. No fish in sight.

Then I thought I better check the fishbowl, just in case. And there was poor Emeril floating belly up, surrounded by bubbles. I saw the pink bottle of bubbles lying on its side beside the fishbowl and screamed, "MOM!"

Emeril was a goner. I knew Ms. Riley was going to be upset and it was all Dylan's fault.

"He ruins everything!" I yelled. "He screws up and I'm the one who gets in trouble. It's bad enough when it happens at home, but now I'll be in trouble at school. I shouldn't have to share my room with a baby. It's not fair."

We had no choice- we had to flush Emeril. But when we brought him into the bathroom, Dylan freaked out and started crying.

"Fishy doesn't have to go potty!" he wailed.

My parents felt bad for *him*. And we had to have a dumb funeral in the backyard. I felt so stupid standing around, watching Dad bury the fish.

Dylan was still crying, saying "I sowwy, Fishy. I didn't mean to huwt you." I might have even felt bad for him, if I wasn't so mad at him for messing with my stuff. That's when I looked up and saw Simon staring out the window. Great, just what I needed- an audience.

CHAPTER 7

R.I.P. Emeril

I really needed a break from my family, so I retreated to my room for a round of Ball Bomb. It's a game Luke and I created. We would see how many times we could bounce my Nerf basketball off the ceiling and catch it, never letting it hit the floor. Now I was flying solo, but I had already broken our old record of seventy-nine bounces and I was going strong. It took my mind off the fish, and Mr. Smith's ankle, and TJ Hinkleman.

I had bounced the ball ninety-five times in a row and I was totally in the zone. And I just knew I could break 100.

Bounce. Ninety-six.

This was a piece of cake.

Bounce. Ninety- seven.

Who needs Luke anyway?

Bounce. Ninety-eight.

Victory would be mine.

Bounce. Ninety-nine.

It was almost too easy.

I could hear the sports announcer shouting my name in his microphone. *Alex Baker, world champion ball bouncer, breaks all records and scores…*

Bounce. One hund…

Then the phone rang and the ball bobbled out of my hands. I reached past my bed, trying to recover it, but it was too late. I clenched my fist, as I watched the ball drop to the floor, hit an empty Pringles can, and roll into my closet.

"Really? Ninety-nine? You've got to be kidding me?" I shouted to myself. I punched my pillow and shook my head, picking up the phone.

"Hello," I huffed into the phone, in a voice that my mother would definitely not consider "good phone manners".

"Hi, Is Alex there?" asked a nasally voice.

"Yeah, it's me," I replied, wondering who this was that broke my almost perfect score of 100 bounces.

"Hi, it's Simon," he said pausing for a second. "You know, the new kid next door. I was wondering if maybe you want to come over for a little bit. I have something that you might want."

I thought to myself, *Something I might want? Like a pain- in-the butt neighbor who makes me drop the ball right when I'm ready to break an all- time record? No thank you!*

I hesitated for a second. "I uh.... I can't right now." I had to think quickly. "I'm trying to finish my homework."

"Oh," he said kind of softly, sounding disappointed. Then he sneezed into the phone and sniffed. "Ok, I understand. Well I guess I'll just see you at school tomorrow."

Something about the way he said that made me feel really bad about blowing him off. I mean it wouldn't kill me to go over his house for little bit. Even if he did make me drop the ball.

"Well... I guess I could come over. Just for a few minutes though."

"Okay," he said, sounding much happier.

"Alright then, see you in a minute," I mumbled.

I headed toward Luke's house, which was now Simon's house. That just felt weird. I rang the doorbell and Simon's mom opened the door. She had long frizzy red hair that looked like a lion's mane and thick glasses like Simon's.

"Oh, hi!" she said, straightening her *Kiss the Cook* apron. "You must be the boy from next door. Alex, right? Simon told me you're in his class. He'll be so happy that you came to visit."

"Simon," she called upstairs. "Your friend is here."

Friend? I thought to myself. *We might be going a bit overboard.*

"Go ahead upstairs. He's in his room, the first door on the left."

"Oh, Luke's room," I said.

She looked puzzled. "No, Simon's room, Dear."

I shrugged my shoulders. "Okay," I replied.

I didn't feel like explaining about Luke.

I headed upstairs and stared at the door. It used to have a sign that said: *Enter at Your Own Risk.* Now it just looked empty.

Simon burst open the door. "Oh, hi, Alex," he said, a big goofy grin on his face. "Come on in."

I hesitated for a moment before I stepped inside. The room looked all wrong. Instead of baseball pennants on the walls, there were alien posters. Instead of trophies lining the dresser, there was a telescope. And instead of Luke's game winning basketball lying in the corner of the room, there was an iguana in a glass tank, his eyes bugging out at me.

Simon rushed over to his desk in the corner of the room. It was covered in colored pencils, crayons, and sketch paper. I guessed he was really into the whole art thing. There was a weird alien drawing on top of a pile of papers, it was a pretty good. It looked like the Alien from Space Warriors, a movie Luke and I went to see before he left.

"What's up, Simon? Did you want to show me something?"

He grabbed a clear plastic bag off his desk and held it out proudly.

"Well, I thought maybe you could use this." A goldfish darted back and forth inside the bag. "I wasn't spying or anything, but I uh…I saw you guys in your yard tonight and I thought maybe you could use a replacement for Emeril."

I shrugged. "I dunno."

It was too much. The room. The iguana. The fish.

It wasn't Luke's room anymore and I was angry about that. I felt like screaming at Simon, telling him to go back to whatever weird place he came from. But then I looked at him, holding out the plastic bag like some sort of peace offering.

I sighed and thought it would be better to bring in a new fish than going to class empty handed. At least Ms. Riley would still have a goldfish.

"I have a bunch in my tank, I don't mind, really," he said.

I glanced at his fish tank on the dresser. There were lots of other fish in there.

"Thanks," I mumbled. "That's uhh….really nice of you." I grabbed the bag and started toward the door, "Well, I guess I'll see you in class."

Simon looked up like he wanted to say something, but then he stopped. "Okay, bye," he said.

I headed downstairs and his mom hurried in from the kitchen.

"Are you leaving so soon? You're welcome to stay for a while. I was just making you guys some snacks. We have cheese popcorn," she offered hopefully.

"Umm... Sorry but I have to go. I have to finish my homework."

I really did have work to do. I wasn't trying to be a total jerk. It was cool that he gave me the fish and all. But as far as being friends, we really just didn't have much in common.

I thought about trying to pass this fish off for Emeril, but he had a black spot on his tail fin and Ms. Riley would know the difference. Besides I wouldn't feel right lying to her. She was a little crazy, but she had a way of growing on you.

For my journal entry, I decided to write an obituary. I kept thinking about how excited Ms. Riley had been about letting us take home Emeril. I hoped that she wouldn't be too sad.

I picked up my pencil and began writing:

Emeril was a good fish. He enjoyed living in our 6th grade classroom at Kennedy School. He liked blowing bubbles and was a huge fan of fish flakes. He recently took a trip to Alex Baker's house where he was involved in a terrible accident involving bubble bath. A short memorial service was held at Alex's house on Friday night. Surviving in class are 2 guinea pigs, 3 frogs, and a tadpole. He will be missed by the 6th grade.

Below the assignment I wrote a note:

Miss Riley,

I'm really sorry about this. I never meant to hurt him, but my little brother always messes with my stuff. I hope that you're not angry. I'll stay after school and sharpen pencils all week if you want me to.

From, Alex

CHAPTER 8

Trouble Brewing

Ms. Riley wasn't mad about Emeril. And she really loved the new fish. When I told her what happened, she said, "I have a younger sister, and I remember what it's like sharing a room. But it's important that you forgive your little brother. Siblings are blessings and someday you'll really appreciate having a little brother."

I sighed and nodded. I had a lot of choice words for Dylan, but "blessing" was not one of them.

She held up the new fish smiling, as she peered into the plastic bag, her eyes growing large, magnified by the clear plastic.

"Ah, yes. We have new member of our 6th grade family. Welcome little fish. I think we'll call you Leonardo. Doesn't he remind you of Leonardo, Alex?" She tilted her head and smiled.

"Um, yeah. I guess so," I stammered. I think she was talking about the famous inventor guy we were studying in Social Studies, and I have absolutely no clue how the fish looked like him. But if it made Ms. Riley happy, I would go with it.

She turned to the class. "Okay, everyone. Let's welcome Leonardo."

"Welcome, Leonardo," the class mumbled. I could hear giggling in the back row.

TJ shouted, "Let's hope this one doesn't get all washed up."

Randy laughed and high-fived him. "Yeah Alex, next time bring your rubber ducky in the tub instead," he added.

I shot him a look. The only thing worse than a bully is a bully's wannabe sidekick.

Then I heard a nasally voice.

"Well, actually...it wasn't Alex's fault."

I looked down row 3 and saw Simon facing TJ. Oh, God. This couldn't be good. In my head I'm screaming, *Shut up, Simon. Just let it go.*

TJ spun around in his seat, his eyes spewing venom. "Who asked you, Bug? You just worry about your own business, like updating that sad wardrobe of yours."

Simon looked down at his notebook, his cheeks turning red.

Ms. Riley stared at TJ, the grin melting from her face. "TJ, that's quite enough. We live in a country where freedom of speech is insured by the Bill of Rights. Perhaps you need to stay after class to review the Constitution." She raised an eyebrow and stared down the aisle.

TJ glared at Simon and then turned back to Ms. Riley. "No, I think I got that covered Ms. Riley. We live in a country where we are all free... even freak shows," he mumbled under his breath.

Simon stared at his shoes and I slid down into my seat, wanting to disappear. Boy, did I wish Luke was here to put TJ in his place.

Later that afternoon, we were on the playground choosing teams for kickball. It was kind of wet, since it had rained the night before and Coach warned us to stay away from the puddles. TJ and Emily were team captains. TJ picked Randy, and Devin. Then he picked me. I wasn't thrilled about being on his team, but at least

I wasn't picked last, like Simon. He stood there between our two teams, glancing back and forth until he was the last guy.

TJ huffed, his face red and sweaty. "Great, I guess that means we're stuck with the bug." At first Simon didn't move.

"Yo, four eyes. Get over here. You're on our team."

Simon met TJ's stare. His eyes narrowed and I thought he was going to say something, but instead he just stared back at TJ.

A silent protest.

"Yo, bug. What's the matter, did you forget your hearing aid? Get over here now."

Simon's feet stayed firmly planted, not budging. I glanced over to see where Coach was, but he was at the door talking to our secretary, Miss Jones, oblivious to the situation. The next thing I knew, TJ was dragging Simon over towards our team. Simon's legs and arms flailed, but he was no match for Hinkleman.

I shouted, "Hey Hinkleman, lay off." I kind of surprised myself. I didn't realize what I was saying. The words just came out.

TJ released Simon and glared at me. "What? Are you friends with this freak?"

Simon looked at me, his eyes searching for an ally.

I looked away and shook my head. "Just give him a break."

Simon's chin started to quiver.

Don't cry, I thought. Don't give him the satisfaction.

"Yeah," Emily spoke up. "Why do you have to be such a jerk, TJ?"

"You want a break, Bug? I'll give you a break." He shoved Simon really hard into a huge puddle on the side of the playground. He landed with a splash and staggered to his feet, covered in muddy water. Even his hair was wet. He stood there looking out from his mud-splattered glasses. I wanted to say something, to help him up, to give him a hand, but I did nothing. I was afraid to say any more.

"And you, Baker. Watch it or you're next."

Finally, Coach came back over. He looked at Simon and asked, "What happened here?"

TJ quickly answered before Simon got the chance to say anything. "He fell in the puddle."

Coach eyed TJ suspiciously. "Is that right, Simon?" Simon stood there for a moment, then he nodded slowly. I watched as a grin crept across TJ's face.

On the bus ride home that afternoon, Danielle said, "That was a decent thing you did today, sticking up for Simon." She laughed and said, "I guess you're not a total jerk, little cousin."

I mumbled, "Gee thanks," but I really didn't feel like I was much of a help. And besides, now I was on TJ's bad side which was a dangerous place to be.

CHAPTER 9

Monster Spray

All I wanted to do when I got home that day was go to my room, watch a little *Captain Destruction*, and have a nice mug of root beer. Was that too much to ask? I guess it was because with the beauty shop in our front room, I never knew who would be there to greet me when I came home.

When I opened the door, I saw someone with red hair sitting under the hair dryer.

Oh, no, I thought. *Here we go.*

I realized the red-haired lady was Simon's mom and I tried to hurry by, but she popped her head out from under the dryer. "Oh, hi honey!" she said, patting her frizzy red mane.

"Hi, Mrs. Connor," I mumbled, heading for the door.

"Well, this is just wonderful! You and Simon are pals and now your mom is my hairdresser. When I found out she cuts hair, I just thanked my lucky stars. Now I can just scoot over here whenever I need this mop trimmed."

"Uh, that's great," I said, almost at the door.

But then Mom said, "Honey, your friend came to visit, too."

I froze. *Oh no. Friend?*

"Simon, come on in here and say hello," Mrs. Connor called.

Simon shuffled into the room, clutching a big frosty mug.

My root beer. Really?

He pushed his glasses up on his nose and took a long sip. He hiccupped and said "Hi, Alex."

Geez, he was sure making himself at home. I mean I felt bad for him and all. I knew he had a rough day. But come on.

My house? My root beer? What's next? Would he be wearing my dino slippers and snuggling with Mr. Fuzzskin? (Not that I snuggled with my teddy bear anymore. I only kept him hidden under my bed in case of emergencies, like really bad thunder storms and scary movies.)

"Hi," I said, eyeing that mug. We kind of stood there silent for a moment. Then he took a big slug of my soda and sneezed, splattering me with root beer.

"Oops, sorry!" he blurted, spraying more soda.

I wiped my face and cracked my knuckles. "Well, I think I'll just head up to my room for a while," I said.

My mom, who was at the sink rinsing someone's hair, looked up and gave me 'the look'. You know the look. The *Don't-Think-You're-Going-To-Get-Away-with-That-Mister* look.

My mom is an expert at that look.

"Well then, Alex. You'll get the chance to show Simon your room. Why don't the two of you go upstairs until we're finished here?" She smiled, but clenched her teeth. And I could tell by her eyes that she meant business.

I sighed. "Okay. Come on, Simon."

Dylan followed us up the stairs. He was dressed in his Batman pajamas, which he'd worn every day that week. He zoomed in my room ahead of us, with his cape flapping behind him.

"Dylan, can't you stay downstairs with mom for a few minutes?" I asked.

"No way! I have to fight the bad guys," he shouted.

Simon looked around with a surprised look on his face. "What bad guys?" he asked.

"Well for starters, he's convinced there's a monster in the closet," I said. "I really wish that Batman here could get him, because he's keeping us awake at night."

Dylan woke me up the night before, screaming about the monster in our closet. He ended up in my bed, kicking me and hogging the covers. To make matters worse, I woke up when I felt something warm and wet creeping across the sheet. He wet *my* bed!

Dylan nodded to Simon, his wide eyes confirming the awful truth. "There's a big haiwy monstew in thawe," Dylan said, pointing towards the closet.

Simon smiled. "There is? Is he green and purple?"

Dylan nodded slowly, sucking his thumb.

"Does he have big yellow horns and three eyes?" he asked, looking almost serious.

Dylan gulped and whispered, "Yes."

"Well, I think I know how you can solve that problem," he said.

"You do?" Dylan asked.

"You do?" I echoed.

Simon crouched down by Dylan and looked him in the eye. He whispered, "A long time ago, there was a monster in my closet."

"Weally?" Dylan asked, his eyes fixed on Simon.

"He scared me all the time, especially at night. Then my dad gave me something that solved my problem."

"What?" asked Dylan.

Simon leaned forward and whispered, "Monster Spray."

Dylan's eyes popped open. "Monstew spway?"

"Yep, monster spray. Monsters are terrified of it. It makes their fur melt. If you spray it, they take off and never come back."

"Do you know where we can get some of that monster spray? We could sure use some," I said.

"I might still have some," he said. "I'll check when I go home." Simon grinned and pushed his glasses up on his nose.

"Hey, sorry about what happened today at school. TJ can be a real jerk sometimes."

Simon nodded. "It's ok. I'm alright."

I realized that he was alright and it was not so bad having Simon as a next-door neighbor.

The next day on the bus, I passed by Danielle and sat next to Simon.

"Hey," I said.

He looked really surprised that I was sitting next to him. And that made me feel bad about ignoring him before. It couldn't be easy being the new kid.

"Hi," he said, rummaging through his book bag. "I have something for you." He pulled out a bottle that said 'Monster Spray'. It had this really cool picture of a three-eyed monster on the label.

"Wow, did you draw this?" I asked.

He nodded. "Yeah, I got an old hairspray bottle and filled it with water. Then I just sketched the label."

"This is good. You can really draw," I said.

"Thanks." He shrugged his shoulders. "I hope it works."

"Me, too," I said. "I could sure use some sleep."

There were no major problems at school that day, probably because TJ was absent. I even survived the mystery meat on a hard roll at lunch and a pop quiz on the continents in Social Studies class. I figured that if I started bringing my own lunch and found out where exactly Australia was, I just might survive 6th grade after all.

CHAPTER 10

Captain Cheeseburger

The weekend had finally arrived and things were looking up. I couldn't believe it, but the "monster spray" actually worked. I handed Dylan the monster spray and said, "Use it carefully, because it's very powerful stuff." I bit my lip, trying not to smile.

Dylan nodded and carefully reached for the bottle. He was in full Batman gear and ready to defeat the enemy. He eyed the monster on the label carefully. Then he nodded and pulled his Batman mask over his eyes. He was on a mission. He rapidly fired the spray, spinning in circles, his little cape flapping behind him. He sprayed inside our closet, under both of our beds, and just about everywhere else in our room. Our carpet was soaked but it was worth it.

"Take that, monstews", he shouted, rapidly spraying the air.

"Hey, Dylan. Listen." I turned my head, sticking out my ear. "I think I can hear them running away," I said, hoping he'd buy it.

He gasped and his eyes popped wide open. "I hear them, too," he whispered. Then he scrunched his face into his best monster fighting scowl and sprayed some more. "BAM, BAM, SHZAM!"

That night, I was able to sleep for the first time in weeks. And the next morning was great. I played some video games, shot a few hoops, and watched an Alien Zombie marathon on TV. It was my kind of Saturday. I should have known things were going a little too well.

Mom came into the living room right at the end of Alien Zombies III, jiggling her car keys and pulling Dylan by the hand. She smiled brightly. "We are going to Burger Boat for lunch. I have a little surprise for you."

Surprise? Last time my parents sprung a little surprise on me, I ended up with a pain-in-the- butt brother. I don't think I could handle another surprise like Dylan. But it didn't help to drill mom for info, she keeps secrets locked up like space pods in Alien Invaders.

So, we piled in the minivan for some quality bonding over fried food and mysterious secret unveiling.

"Where's Dad?" I asked, wondering why he wasn't coming with us.

"Uh... you'll see soon," Mom replied.

Something wasn't adding up here. Why would Mom tell us a big secret without Dad around? *Could they be getting a divorce like Luke's parents?* I wondered. *Could it be because he lost his job?*

"I want Daddy," Dylan whined, twirling his Brady dinosaur around by the tail. He was swinging it really close to the open window.

"You better stop swinging that mutant lizard near the window," I said.

"He's not a wizard. He's my best fwiend." Dylan smiled. And don't worwy, Alex. He can fly, see?"

He held Brady outside of the window, making zooming airplane sounds.

"Dylan, NO!" I yelled, but it was too late.

He dropped Brady out the window right at the intersection of Main Avenue and Luzerne Street.

I spun around and stared out the back window. There was Brady, that same crazy grin on his face, lying belly up amid cars whizzing by in both lanes.

"Ummm, Mom. You might want to pull over."

Dylan started screaming and pounding his fists on the arms of his car seat.

"I need Bwady! Someone help Bwady! He bwoke his leg!" he wailed.

Mom glanced out her side view mirror and sighed, pulling over to the side of the road.

"Really? Alex, couldn't you keep an eye on your brother for the five-minute ride to Burger Boat? Honestly, sometimes it's hard to remember that you're twelve."

I shook my head in disbelief. "I really can't believe you're blaming me for this."

"It's okay, Baby. Alex will go get Brady for you. Won't you Alex?" Mom said, nodding toward me.

"Yeah, sure. Let me go leap into oncoming traffic to risk my life for a dumb purple dinosaur."

"Alright, just remember to look both ways," she replied.

"Gee, Mom. Thanks for your concern." I shook my head and sighed.

I jumped out of the van and when the light turned red I hurried over to scoop up the dinosaur, but when I leaned over my baseball hat fell off and blew into the oncoming traffic lane. And then a bus ran over my hat.

My favorite OverArmour baseball hat, that I saved my allowance for 3 weeks to buy, now had a big muddy tire print right down the middle. A dirty skunk stripe.

Just my luck. The creepy dinosaur survived and my hat was ruined. I grabbed Brady by the throat ready to ring his purple neck. I stared into his beady eyes, shaking him violently.

"See what you did?" I screamed.

I looked up just in time to see Emily riding by on her bike. She looked a little concerned, but managed to smile.

"Uh... Hi Alex. Nice Dino."

"Oh, thanks," I mumbled, straightening my muddy cap on my head. *Great, now she thinks I'm a psycho dinosaur strangler*, I thought.

I didn't say a word for the rest of the ride.

When we pulled into the parking lot, I saw Dad's white truck parked near the door. I knew it was his because it had an 'I LOVE CATS' sticker on the bumper, which is pretty ironic because he hates cats, but he loved the deal that he got at Big John's Used Cars.

"Why is Dad here?" I asked slowly, with a sense of impending doom.

"You'll see," mom replied. A weird grin crept across her face.

I trudged across the parking lot, palms sweating and heart pounding. Then I opened the door and saw him... in a cheesy striped shirt, sporting an eye patch and a stuffed parrot on his shoulder.

Dad was the new Captain Cheeseburger.

"Ahoy there, Bakers!" I heard him bellow over the pirate music pumping through the speakers. He smiled from behind the cash register. "Can I interest you in a Skipper Meal?"

Yep. Things just kept getting worse.

I had to do something to help Dad, so that evening I mailed the apology letter to my dad's old boss. I was determined to help him get his job back before anyone found out about his new career move. I couldn't bear the thought of my friends finding out about his job, not for all the fries in Burger Boat.

CHAPTER 11

Skipper Meals and Saddle Shoes

On Monday morning, I knew I was in trouble as soon as I walked into the classroom and saw the boat-shaped box on my desk.

A Skipper Meal.

How did it get there? What did it mean?

Then I heard the laughing. I looked up and there was TJ, staring at me with a big cocky grin on his face. Panic swept over me. My little secret was about to be revealed.

"Ahoy, Baker. I went to Burger Boat last night and they had a new skipper on board. Your Daddy is a real pro at slinging burgers. He's very talented. And he looks really cool in the dorky striped shirt and sailor hat."

TJ's dad had worked as a custodian at my Dad's insurance office. I guess he found out about my Dad getting laid off and was trying to rub it in. I stood there in shock.

"You're really stepping up in the world. Your Daddy's is rockin' that pirate patch and you've made a really cool friend." He nodded toward Simon who was sitting at his desk, staring at him, his eyes bugging out behind his thick glasses.

"Shut up, TJ," I whispered, teeth clenched.

"Hey everyone, I have an announcement to make. Alex's Dad is now a proud employee of Burger Boat. He makes a mean

Skipper Meal. Right, Small Fry." He laughed so hard that he was snorting and turning red. "Get it, Small Fry?"

Randy snickered.

I smiled and tried to act like I didn't care, but I could feel my cheeks burning.

Just then, Ms. Riley entered the room and announced a pop quiz. I don't think I'd ever been happier to reduce fractions. It bought me some time, but I had a sinking feeling that TJ's tirade had only just begun.

During recess, we were playing keep away, when Michael McDonnell knocked the ball away from TJ and it rolled towards Simon. He was sitting under a tree reading his Space Pod comic book.

Simon kicked it away, just as TJ was running over to get it.

"Yo Bug, you trying to kick that ball away from me? Keep your dorky shoes off that ball. If you want to play keep away, I'll show you how the game is played."

Suddenly he yanked at Simon's shoe and he pulled it off. Simon looked up, shocked. He struggled to move away, but TJ pulled his other shoe off just as quickly.

Simon sprung to his feet and shouted, "Give them back, TJ."

"Try to make me." TJ was off and running, swinging the shoes in the air. "It's keep away from the dork."

He tossed the shoes to Michael, who laughed and threw them back.

Simon stood near the tree in his striped socks, motionless. I knew he needed help. The lunch ladies were talking at the other end of the playground and didn't realize what was happening.

I ran after TJ, shouting, "Leave him alone, you jerk."

TJ stopped and looked at me for a minute. Then he smiled, "Well, well, well. It looks like Small Fry is sticking up for his new buddy, Big Dork. Isn't that sweet?"

He fumbled with the laces, quickly tying them together.

"I suppose you want these," he said swinging them above his head. Then he tossed the shoes high up in the air towards a telephone line that ran near the edge of the playground. The shoes fell and I tried to catch them, but I missed. He tossed them two more times until finally he looped them over the line. The shoes dangled high on the wire, swaying in the wind.

I glanced at Simon, still standing near the tree. He looked like he couldn't take much more.

My heart was pounding. I knew I had to do something. It just wasn't right. He had to be stopped. Now was the moment. I took a deep breath and shouted, "WHY ARE YOU SUCH A JERK?

TJ spun around and stared at me, a surprised look on his face. I knew I was about to set him off, a danger signal was exploding in my brain, but I was too fired up to stop now.

"You think you're so tough just 'cause you bully people. Pick on the new kid who doesn't have any friends. Pick on the kid whose dad lost his job. What's next? Are you going to kick some puppies on the way home? You're not cool, you're just a mean jerk."

TJ clenched his jaw and stared at me. I think he was shocked that I actually stood up to him.

Someone shouted, "Yeah, TJ. Not cool, Man."

By this time a crowd of kids had gathered round and the lunch ladies were hurrying over. They took Simon to the office to call home for new shoes. I wondered if he had any other shoes to wear.

When we were lining up to go back inside, TJ came up behind me and leaned over my shoulder. I could feel his hot Dorito breath on my neck as he hissed in my ear, "Watch your back, Small Fry. You're next."

The rest of the afternoon I didn't feel so good. I felt like I had a hundred fifty-pound weight pressing on my stomach. And that weight had a name-TJ Hinkleman. I kept wondering what he would do next. Maybe I should have kept my big mouth shut. But Simon really needed help and somebody had to do stand up to TJ.

Too bad it had to be me.

CHAPTER 12

The Truth about Simon

I didn't eat much during supper. I still didn't feel so well. I took a few nibbles and just pushed the noodles around on my plate.

"Alex, aren't you going to finish your lasagna?" Mom asked. "It's your favorite."

"Uh… I'm not really hungry right now. Maybe I'll have more later."

"Well, how about when we're finished, we go shoot some hoops," Dad asked.

"Me, too," Dylan chimed in

Dad smiled, "Yes, you can play, too."

"How 'bout you guys start without me. I'm going over to Simon's for a little while. I have to ask him something." I cleared my plate and headed for the door.

"Oh, Mom. Where did you put my old high tops?"

Mom gave me a strange look, not sure what I was up to. "They should be on your closet shelf."

"Thanks," I called, running upstairs.

When I rang the bell at Simon's house, his mom answered the door. She really didn't seem like herself. No bright smile. No overly friendly greeting. No cheese popcorn.

"Hi, Mrs. Connor. Is Simon here?"

"Yeah, he's upstairs. Go ahead up, but go easy on him, Alex. He's having a hard day."

Simon was sitting at his desk sketching some aliens in a battle scene. They were really good. There was a green alien with three eyes battling a purple creature with horns and huge fangs.

"Wow, that's really good," I said.

"Thanks." His eyes looked red and puffy, like he had been crying. "Well...I get plenty of practice. There's nothing else to do around here."

"You know, you could come over and shoot hoops with us. Sometimes my Dad and I shoot around after supper."

"I don't think I'd be very good. I never played much," he said, wiping his nose.

I laughed. "I'm no all-star either. You'd be in good company."

He smiled just a little. "Thanks, maybe I will."

"Listen, sorry about how TJ acted today. He can be such a jerk. I don't know what he's trying to prove. Anyway, you helped me out with the fish and the monster spray. Now I'd like to return the favor." I laughed. "You know the whole karma thing that Miss Riley always talks about."

I held up the slightly worn, neon green high tops and said, "I hope they fit. They're not brand new, but they're not too bad."

He smiled and said, "Thanks."

"Just think, it will give you the chance to try a new style. Hang up those saddle shoes and try some high tops. Get it? *Hang up* the saddle shoes?" I grinned, hoping to cheer him up, but he didn't smile.

Wow, my jokes were lame.

"You must have really liked those shoes, huh?" I asked.

He breathed a heavy sigh and said, "It's just that, they belonged to my Dad. I found them in our attic before we moved here, and when I tried them on, they fit just right." He blinked and stared down at his sketch book. "I know it sounds dumb, but I feel like when I wear them, he's not too far away."

"Oh," I said, thinking about those shoes. I never realized they had a special meaning to him.

"Where's your Dad now?" I asked, a little scared that I was butting into his business.

Simon looked down at his sketch. "He died last year." He sighed and wiped his nose. "He was sick for a long time."

"Oh, wow. I'm really sorry, Simon. I had no idea."

"He fought hard and he always tried to look happy, even in the end. But I knew he was suffering. Mom pulled me out of school when I was in second grade and home-schooled me. She wanted to keep our family together for the time he had left."

I wasn't sure what to say, but it seemed like he wanted to talk so I asked, "What was he like?"

He was quiet for a minute, kind of lost in his own world. Then he looked up and said, "He was a college professor and an amazing artist. He always snorted when he laughed. He loved science fiction movies and cold spaghetti sandwiches."

He shook his head and laughed.

"He used to take me to his university. Sometimes he let me help teach class. I would use the laser pointer to point out the bones in the dinosaurs displayed on the projector. His students called me 'Little Professor'."

He was quiet for a minute. Then he whispered, "I really miss him."

"Sounds like he was a great guy," I replied, thinking about my own Dad and how lucky I was to have him, pirate patch and all.

"I think that's why it's kind of hard for me," he replied. "I'm not used to school and being around kids- it's all new to me. I just never know what to do or say."

"Things will get better." I shrugged. "People just have to get to know you."

He shook his head. "I'm not like you, Alex. I don't dress cool. I don't know how to talk to other kids. I don't know how to speak up for myself."

I was really surprised that he thought those things came easy to me.

"You've already got a friend." I patted him on the shoulder. "And things will get easier, you'll see. You've just got to believe in yourself and other people will, too."

I was kind of surprised by the words coming out of my mouth. But I think it was good advice and I somehow felt a little stronger saying it to Simon.

Later that night, I shot some hoops with my Dad and Dylan. I even sunk a few 3 pointers. I was definitely getting better. It was kind of nice having my Dad around more often. His work hours were much better since he started working at the restaurant. I couldn't imagine what my life would be like without him. And even Dylan, who drove me crazy sometimes, could be a pretty cool little guy.

I suddenly realized what Luke had meant when he said I was lucky. I held Dylan up so he could do a slam dunk.

"He shoots, he scores!" I shouted.

Dylan clapped and yelled, "Yay! I shot it up high in the sky." Hearing those words gave me a great idea.

CHAPTER 13

The Long Shot

I hopped on my bike with my basketball perched between the handle bars, and raced over to the school. It was getting dark, and a little hard to see, but sure enough Simon's shoes were still dangling high on the telephone wire.

I stood right below the shoes and shot the ball as far as I could. No luck. I tried again. The ball crashed down on the pavement again and again. I was worried someone was going to kick me off the playground for trespassing after dark. Then I heard footsteps behind me. I spun around and there was Emily, walking her black lab, Pepper.

"Hey, Alex. What are you doing?" she asked.

I felt my cheeks burning. "Well, I uhh... I was just trying to hit Simon's shoes off the wire. I guess it's kind of a long shot."

"I don't know why TJ did that. He's acting like a real moron this year." She paused and nodded. "But it was nice that you stuck up for Simon."

"I didn't do much," I said, kicking a stone on the playground.

"But at least you did something," she added, smiling.

Then Pepper lunged forward, trying to chase after a squirrel.

"Well, good luck. I hope you hit your target." She called over her shoulder, as she jogged after Pepper.

"Thanks," I said.

I hoped I wasn't too sweaty from shooting at the wire for the last twenty minutes. I stood back and aimed one more time. I was either going to get those shoes down or knock out all the phone connections in the area-whichever came first. Then I heard a smack against the pavement.

And there they were sitting on the pavement, laces still tied together. I never thought I'd be so happy to see an old pair of saddle shoes.

"Yes!" I shouted and I hopped up in triumph. I snatched the shoes, draped them over my handlebars, and headed for Simon's house. I left them on his porch with a note that said:

Here are your shoes. Can't wait to see the look on TJ's face when he sees you wearing them tomorrow!
Your friend, Alex

CHAPTER 14

Hinkleman Strikes Again

The next day, Simon climbed aboard the bus wearing those saddle shoes and a million-dollar grin. I slid over to make room for him.

"Looking good, Simon," I said, nodding to his shoes.

"Thanks."

"No problem," I replied.

"But how did you…?" he asked.

"Let's just say I've been working on my long shot."

"Oh," he said, looking puzzled.

When we walked into our classroom, T.J. and Randy were standing in the back trying to act like big shots in front of Emily. T.J. was bragging about how he scored a touchdown during a game on Saturday morning. Emily rolled her eyes and walked away.

When she saw me, she smiled.

"It looks like your aim is not so bad," she said, eyeing Simon's shoes.

TJ followed her gaze and his mouth dropped open. Then he looked at me and his surprise melted into anger. I don't know how he figured out that I got the shoes back. Maybe it was just a lucky guess or maybe it was my game-winning grin. But he pieced it together and he almost burned a hole right through my forehead with his stare. I didn't even blink. I just glared right back at him.

"Well, Baker," he began. "It looks like you just moved up a few more notches on the dork-o-meter, rescuing your new best buddy. Maybe you can get a pair of those cool shoes, too. Then you could be dork twins."

"Lay off, T.J.," I replied, unpacking my books.

He leaned real close and whispered in my ear. "Don't mess with me, Baker. Your buddy isn't here to protect you anymore."

He cracked his knuckles and strutted back to his seat, with Randy chuckling behind him.

I stayed clear of TJ for the rest of the day. In the hall, I hurried to my next class and at lunchtime I hung out with Simon. We sat at a bench near the front of the playground, not far from the lunch ladies.

He showed me his sketchbook and the kid blew me away.

"Woah! These are awesome. Dude, you can seriously draw." There were pictures of aliens, dragons, and other cool creatures. And I swear, they looked like they were straight out of a book.

"Are you sure you didn't trace these?" I asked

Simon shook his head.

"Really, Dude. These are good."

He shrugged and smiled. "Thanks."

Just before it was time to go in, Simon had to use the bathroom. The lunch ladies opened the door and let him in. I saw TJ watching from across the playground, and wouldn't you know it, he made a bee line for the door. The lunch lady shook her head. I guess she didn't want a bunch of kids using the bathroom at the same time. But then he started hopping up and down and making this face like it was a real emergency, and she bought it. I watched him disappear into the building. I knew that meant trouble.

They wouldn't let me in the building, too. And to be honest, I was a little afraid to go in. So, there was nothing to do but wait. It felt like an hour before the bell finally rang, signaling the end of recess. I grabbed Simon's sketch book and put it in my backpack. When we headed inside, there was still no sign of Simon. I took a detour down the side hall and circled back to the boys' lav. I could hear Simon yelling as soon as I opened the door.

"Help!"

The stall door was swinging slightly open and I saw two sets of feet behind it, one wearing saddle shoes.

I heard TJ, "Come on bug. Let's wash that hair of yours." He was pushing Simon's head toward the toilet. I dropped my bag and ran over to the stall.

"Let him go, TJ" I shouted.

He craned his neck towards me and smiled.

"You want to go next?" he asked, his face red and sweaty.

I pulled his arm to let Simon go, but he just pushed harder. Simon looked at me, his eyes begging for help. His head was getting dangerously close to the toilet.

Just then Randy burst in the door and started laughing. "Alright! Dunk the dork!" he yelled.

I didn't know what to do. I knew I was no match for the two of them. I did the only thing I thought could help at the moment. I ran out in the hall and looked for the nearest teacher. That might sound like a wimpy thing to do, but I knew I was no match for TJ and Randy.

I found Principal Johnson at the end of the hall.

"Mr. Johnson, come quick," I said trying to catch my breath. "They've got Simon in the bathroom."

Mr. Johnson hurried down the hall and flung the door open, but we were too late. Simon sat in the corner, holding his head in his hands. His hair was dripping. He looked up, and the beads of water rolled off his glasses.

"Sorry, Man" I whispered. I handed him some paper towels. "I tried to get help."

He grasped some soggy papers in his hands. They were drawings from his sketchbook. They must have doused it, too.

"I'm alright," he said, wiping his face with the paper towels. He nodded toward the stall. "Alex, they got your back pack, too."

I glanced in the stall and saw it wedged in the toilet.

"Who did this to you, son?" Mr. Johnson asked, a concerned look on his face.

Simon sat there quietly. Then he shook his head and mumbled, "I don't know. I think they were eighth graders."

Mr. Johnson turned toward to me. "Is that right, Alex? Do you know them?"

I glanced at Simon. He shook his head, signaling for me to stay quiet. I guess he didn't want to rat on TJ. I'm not sure that was a smart move.

Mr. Johnson stared at me, his eyes narrowed. "Are you sure you don't know them, Alex?"

I hesitated a moment, knowing that we should probably tell. But then I just shook my head.

"If you see these kids again, come let me know. No one has the right to treat you this way. Come on, Son."

He helped Simon up and took him to the office. They were probably calling his mom to come and get him again. He had to be so embarrassed.

I fished my book bag out of the toilet. The bottom was completely waterlogged. I opened it up and tossed my soggy folder and notebooks in the garbage. I thought about throwing away the whole stupid backpack, but I knew my mom would give me a hard time with money being tight. Besides, I really didn't want to tell her what happened.

CHAPTER 15

Secrets Revealed

When I came home that day, I heard a familiar voice in the beauty shop. Mrs. Kimble, my second-grade teacher, was sitting under the hair dryer holding a stack of math worksheets in her lap. When she saw me walk in, she smiled.

"Hi Alex, how are you doing?"

Suddenly I felt like I was in second grade again. "Hi, Mrs. Kimble. I'm doing good."

"You mean well, Dear. You're doing well," she corrected.

"Uh, yeah. I'm well."

"That's good, Dear."

Before I could escape to my room, mom called me back to the shop.

"Alex, I need you to watch your brother for me. I'll be done here in a few minutes. He's in the living room. Just make sure he doesn't get into trouble."

I was ready to protest, but since Mrs. Kimble was there, I felt like I might get sent to the principal's office.

"Okay," I mumbled, heading into the next room.

Dylan was there watching Brady on TV. Ugh. What a way to end the day, curling up on the couch to watch a dumb purple dinosaur dance around on TV. I knew if I changed the channel there would be a major melt down, so I sucked it up.

"Hi, Monster," I called to Dylan.

He didn't even answer me. He was frozen in front of the T.V screen, mesmerized by the giant purple reptile. A few minutes later Dylan started to hop around and jiggle, his bat man cape flapping up and down. I knew what that meant. He had to use the potty, but prying him away from Brady was harder than blasting zombies in Alien Invaders.

"Dylan, why don't you take a potty break?" I asked.

No answer, just more jumping up and down. I knew we were running out of time.

"Dylan, come on. It will only take a second."

"No," he shouted. "I don't have to go!"

"If you don't go, I'm going to get, Mom" I said, knowing that she'd probably be angry at me for not handling it, but it was better than him having an accident.

As I headed back towards the shop, I could hear Mrs. Kimble saying good-by to my mom.

"Okay, Dear. I'll see you soon," she said. "I have to hurry over to the library to work with the Hinkleman boy. I've been tutoring him after school for 2 years now, but it doesn't help. That poor child just can't learn to read."

I froze in my tracks.

T.J. Hinkleman couldn't read?

I couldn't believe what I was hearing. Sure, I knew he wasn't an honor roll student, but he couldn't read? We were in 6th grade, everyone knew how to read. Then I thought about how he always fooled around during class. If the teacher called on him, he goofed off until she called on someone else. In fact, I couldn't remember him ever reading in front of the class.

And that's when I knew I had him.

That night I thought about how I could use this new information to my advantage. I know it sounds mean, but TJ deserved what he had coming to him. The plan I devised was pretty simple. Show up early to school. Sneak in the classroom before anyone was there. And write in huge letters on the board:

TJ HINKLEMAN IS SO STUPID THAT HE CAN'T READ THIS SENTENCE.
MAYBE THAT'S WHY HE ACTS LIKE SUCH A JERK.

By the time Ms. Riley entered the room, everyone would have read the message and they'd know the truth. TJ would be the only one clueless about what was written on the board, which would prove my point. Instant payback for all the times he humiliated me, or Simon, or anyone else in our class. And I couldn't wait to see the look on his face.

CHAPTER 16

The Showdown

I arrived early to school the next morning. The doors were locked and the kids were outside playing kickball in the schoolyard. Mr. Freeman, the gym teacher, was watching them. I knew this was my chance.

I walked over and said, "Hi, Mr. Freeman."

"Mornin', Alex. How's it going? Still playing basketball?"

"I'm trying. I'm still working on my long shot."

"Stick with it kid, try-outs are in November. You might not be as big as your buddy, Luke, but you've got heart. You're a good player. I'd like to see you on the team."

I was really surprised to hear him say that.

"Thanks, Coach. I'll be there." I said smiling, almost forgetting about the plan. "Uh…I have to use the bathroom. Can I go inside for a minute?"

"Sure, kid." He jiggled the keys on the large ring until he found the right one.

"Here you go." He opened the door and the plan fell into place.

It was almost too easy.

I slipped down the dark hallway and past the teacher's lounge. I could see a light on and hear the buzz of the copy machine. I would have to be careful, someone was in there. I ducked down when I passed by the window.

I stepped inside the dark classroom and picked up a white board marker. I was straining to see the board when suddenly the lights flipped on. My heart seemed to stop. I looked over and there he was. T.J. was standing in the doorway with that cocky grin on his face.

"Well, well, well. What do we have here? Looks like Small Fry is sneaking around a dark classroom. Seems to me you're up to no good. Maybe we should tell Ms. Riley that we have a prowler."

He must have seen me come in and followed me from the playground. I had to think fast or the plan would be ruined.

"Uh… I left my folder here, and I just ran in to get it. I have to finish my math homework," I stammered.

"Wrong. Try again. What were you doing with the marker, Baker? Maybe you were writing a love note to Emily."

"Lay off, T.J.," I said, trying hard to stay calm.

"Maybe you were taking orders for lunch at Burger Boat. Sign me up for a Captain Burger. We have to keep your Daddy busy."

I could feel my cheeks burning. "Shut up, T.J."

"Too bad he can't find a real job. Maybe singing pirate songs is all he can handle."

That was it. I had enough. I was so mad that I was shaking. I took a deep breath and said, "Maybe I was about to tell the whole class about how *stupid* you are. Maybe I know your little secret."

TJ stared at me. His eyes narrowed. I could tell I had his attention.

I looked him in the eye and fired away.

"Maybe you'll shut up when everyone finds out that YOU… CAN'T… READ!"

T.J. turned really red and clenched his fists. For a minute I thought he was going to pound me, but I didn't care. I was done running from him. I was not afraid any more.

Suddenly the bell rang and voices filled the hallway. This was my chance to put him in his place. But then I saw his mouth quiver. He looked like he was going to cry.

T.J. Hinkleman was going to cry.

"Please," he whispered. "Don't tell them."

He was blinking back the tears. Suddenly he didn't seem so tough. And I knew I had the power. I could go in for the kill. Blast him away like an alien zombie.

I hesitated for a moment, staring hard at him. Still angry, but filled with something else, too. I knew that if I humiliated him, it would make me just as bad as him. A bully. And that's not who I wanted to be. I could hear voices in the hall and knew the kids would be here any minute.

TJ sniffed, his shoulders shaking.

I shook my head and sighed. "I won't tell them."

TJ looked at me, surprised. "Do you...do you promise?"

I nodded. "But you have to lay-off, Simon. Cut him some slack." I thought for a minute, then added, "And leave my Dad alone, too."

He nodded slowly and whispered, "Okay."

The kids were rushing into the room now. We headed back to our seats. I wondered if I made the right choice.

I realized that maybe there was more to TJ Hinkleman than meets the eye. Maybe that's true for all of us.

CHAPTER 17

The Bologna Missile

During lunch that day, TJ shuffled over to our table, staring at his feet. His face was bright red. He bit his lip and looked at Simon.

"Yo, man. I just wanted to say...uh..." He was cracking his knuckles and swaying back and forth.

Was he going to apologize? I couldn't believe my ears.

"It's just that I'm uhh... I'm sorry...for givin' you a hard time and all." Then he punched Simon in the shoulder kind of playfully and said, "You're not so bad."

Simon was in the middle of chewing his bologna sandwich and when he heard TJ apologize, he almost choked on a chunk of bologna. He started huffing like he couldn't breathe and I had to give him a quick swat on the back to set that sucker free. The gooey pink lump of bologna shot out of his mouth and hit TJ right between the eyes.

A bologna missile.

I couldn't help it. I started laughing uncontrollably. Simon had a look of horror on his face.

TJ clenched his fists like he was ready to let him have it, but then he glanced at me and groaned. He cracked his knuckles again and headed back to his table, shaking his head and mumbling to himself.

Randy was waiting, his mouth hanging open so wide he could catch a few flies. I heard him say, "Why didn't ya let him have it?"

"Shut up," TJ hissed, punching him on the shoulder, not so playfully.

CHAPTER 18

A Dangerous Meeting

For a while, things were really great. TJ steered clear of me and Simon. Simon had no clue about what brought on the sudden change, but I think he was just glad to be out of the line of fire. And I kept my word and didn't tell anyone about TJ's secret.

I was proud of myself for handling the situation on my own, even without Luke around to save the day. And I was walking a little taller, literally. I had grown almost 2 inches since summer. I was still the shortest kid in class, but every inch counted, especially with basketball tryouts coming up that month.

But I had a funny feeling it wouldn't last. I was glad that T.J. backed off, but I kept waiting for him to strike back. I was always looking over my shoulder and waiting for him to show up at my locker. And then one day, he did.

I had stayed after school to help Ms. Riley carry some things to her car. After the whole Emeril episode, I figured I owed her.

I was coming back in the building to grab my backpack when I saw him there, leaning against my locker. I was ready to dart out the door, but he already spotted me and I didn't want to look like a big wuss. And besides, I knew that he could catch me if he really wanted to. So, I took a deep breath, put on a brave face, and walked over.

"Yo, Baker," he said, nodding in my direction.

"What's up, TJ?" I asked, noticing that he looked a little strange.

"I uhhh…. I need your help with something."

"Help?" I asked.

Help TJ. Why would I want to do that?

This is the guy who gave my book bag a whirlpool bath in the toilet. Keeping his secret was one thing, but actually helping him was another matter altogether. But he had that same look on his face, like when I found out he couldn't read. And I couldn't help it, I kind of felt sorry for him.

I sighed. "What do you need?"

"Meet me at the park at 6 o'clock and I'll explain… And come alone," he huffed.

Come alone? Did he think I was crazy? He probably just wanted a chance to rough me up without any witnesses around.

He could probably tell what I was thinking because he said, "Yo, Baker. Don't have a hissy fit. I'm not going to hurt you. I just need your help."

I don't know why I decided to go to the park that night, but I did. I rode my bike up to the courts where he was shooting hoops and parked it by the fence.

"Hey, Baker. How 'bout we play a little one on one."

"Sure," I said, jogging out on the court. Maybe he wasn't about to pummel me after all.

I watched him dribble for a minute, and then I swooped in and stole the ball.

TJ's eyebrows shot up in surprise. "Whoa, looks like you've been practicing since last year. You were lucky if you ever got your hands on the ball before."

I had been shooting hoops with Dad a lot since he started working at the restaurant. The hours were better and he was home a lot more. I have to admit that I was beginning to like Dad's new job, striped uniform and all.

"You going out for the team this year?" he asked.

"I might," I said, shooting the ball. I watched it bounce off the rim. TJ chuckled and grabbed the rebound, easing it into the net.

I sighed. "Then again, I might not."

We played for a little longer before I finally asked, "Why do you need my help?"

"Well, it's my brother Leroy. I haven't seen him in a while. See he's ...uhhh...he's in jail."

My eyes popped open. "In jail?" I asked.

TJ nodded. His face was all red and sweaty, and he was breathing really hard. I don't know if he was just out of breath or embarrassed. I think maybe it was both.

"Oh," I said, confused.

"Well, you see my old man doesn't want us to visit him. He's really mad at him. Says he's a bad influence."

"Uh-huh," I said, nodding.

I had to take a minute to let it all sink in. TJ's brother, Leroy Hinkleman- star quarterback, was in jail and TJ's dad wouldn't even let him visit him. The kid had things worse than I thought.

TJ stared down at the pavement. "I haven't seen him in a month and I just wanted to write him a letter to say 'hi', so he doesn't...you know...forget about me."

"Sorry to hear about your brother, TJ. But what does all this have to do with me?"

"Since you know about my...uh... my problem, I thought maybe you could write the letter for me." He bit his lip, looking down at his feet.

I knew what a jerk he had been and how easy it would have been to say no. But I thought about how crummy this kid's life was. He couldn't read and he had to hide it from the world. His brother was in jail. And he had to keep up this tough guy act.

I shrugged, thinking that I was probably crazy.

"Yeah, I can help you," I said.

"Good. Come over my house tomorrow after school," he said, grabbing the basketball and jogging toward the parking lot.

"Okay," I mumbled, wondering what I had just gotten myself into.

"And Baker, you're not such a bad player- for a midget and all," he called over his shoulder.

"Gee, thanks, TJ."

"No really, you should try out for the team."

"Maybe I will."

CHAPTER 19

Home Sweet Hinkleman

The next day I headed to TJ's house after school. He only lived two blocks away, so it wasn't a far walk. When we walked up on the porch, you could hear the TV blaring through the screen door. His dad was sitting in a recliner watching game shows in his boxer shorts. He had a beer can in one hand and the remote control in the other. A Basset Hound was snoring at his feet.

"Hi, Pop," TJ said as we walked in the room.

"Uh," he grunted in reply. "There's too many commercials on this dang channel." Then he looked up, surprised to see us. "Why aren't you in school?" he demanded.

"It's 3:30, Pop. School's over."

"Oh," he grunted as he flipped through the channels. "Then you should be doin' your homework. Maybe then you could get something through that thick skull of yours. You want to end up total bum like your brother?

TJ didn't answer. He just shuffled down the hall, mumbling, "Welcome to the Hinkleman castle. Home of happily–ever-after."

I didn't know whether I should laugh or not, so I just kind of snorted.

TJ's room was plastered with posters of motorcycles and monster trucks. He had a lava lamp on his dresser and a pile of dirty clothes in the middle of the floor. I noticed the electric guitar standing in the corner by his night stand, and for some reason that surprised me.

"Hey, you play guitar?" I asked.

"Yeah a little bit. Leroy showed me a few chords," he said, getting that sad look again.

We were both quiet for a minute. Then I asked, "What did he go to jail for anyway?"

"Drinking and driving. And then he mouthed off to the officer. Resisting arrest made things ten times worse. That's why he ended up in the slammer."

"Oh, that's too bad."

I tried to change the subject. "Are you playing your guitar in the talent show?"

Ms. Riley planned a talent show every year before Winter break. Any interested sixth graders got to perform before the whole school.

"No way, Dude. I couldn't play in front of all those kids. Anyway, the whole show is lame. Are you entering it?"

"No, I don't really have much talent. Besides, the idea of standing on that stage in front of everyone freaks me out."

TJ flopped on his bed and started digging through his book bag.

"Here's some paper, Dude. Could you write some stuff down for me?"

"Yep," I said, grabbing a pencil off his desk.

"I couldn't stand the thought of asking Miss Kimble for help," he said, shaking his head.

"Yeah, I bet," I replied.

"That old bat just doesn't get it. She treats me like I'm still in second grade. She tells me to try harder and I'll be able to read those stupid words."

He clenched his fists, his face red. "She just thinks I'm dumb."

I shook my head. "You're not dumb. Maybe you just need someone else to help you."

"Yeah, and let someone else know what a moron I am. I don't think so."

"Well it's up to you, but this whole tough guy act doesn't really fix your problem."

He stared at me for a long time, first all angry, then his face dropped. "Yeah well…I don't know what else to do."

I thought about it for a moment, then said, "I think I know someone who could help you."

CHAPTER 20

Cheese Popcorn to the Rescue

Simon had told me that his mom used to be a teacher before she started home-schooling him. In fact, she used to be a reading specialist. He said that's the kind of teacher who helps people who have reading problems. I called him when I got home that night and told him about TJ's problem.

"I bet my mom could help," he said.

Just like that. No hesitation. No thinking about it. You have to hand it to the kid. He didn't hold a grudge. Somehow, I knew he wouldn't.

The next day, TJ rode home on the bus with us. When Danielle saw the three of us sitting in the back together, she stared at us like she was witnessing an alien invasion. Her mouth hung open and her eyes looked like they were ready to pop right out of her head.

I looked at her and smiled. "Hey Danielle, why don't you take a picture. It would last longer."

"Oh, that's really original, Alex," she replied.

"Thanks," I said, thinking of what a strange team the three of us made.

When we got to Simon's house, his mother was waiting for us, cheese popcorn and all. She even made chocolate chip cookies and had them waiting on the table.

It's really funny how things turn out. If you told me at the beginning of the year that I'd be sitting in Simon's kitchen having chocolate chip cookies with him and TJ, I would have never believed it.

After we were done eating, I went outside with Simon to shoot some hoops. He wasn't very good. He actually made me look like a pro. But he was getting better.

TJ came out to join us a little later. He grabbed the ball.

"Hey, Simon. Your mom's okay, Dude." He shot the ball and sunk it in the net.

"Thanks," Simon said, pushing his glasses up on his nose and grinning.

"She said if I stop by on Friday afternoons, she'll keep helping me."

Simon smiled. "That sounds good, TJ. I'm glad she can help."

I looked at Simon and this time I didn't notice those glasses or jeans, or shoes. This time I just thought about what a good friend he was and how he helped all of us change a little bit. He got me to stand up for myself and be a whole lot braver. He helped my brother get rid of the monster in his closet. He helped TJ drop his tough guy act and got him help when he needed it. He was a really good friend, and I was glad he was there.

I watched as he tried to slap the ball away from TJ, and totally missed. He smiled and started laughing. He was terrible at basketball, but he was having fun. We all were.

CHAPTER 21

Tadpole Poop

After that day, things were different. The three of us started to hang out more often. TJ was learning fast and with Mrs. Connor's help, he was writing his own letters to his brother. Leroy was released on probation a few weeks later. I still don't think TJ had it easy at home, but at least Leroy was there to watch out for him. And he was spending a lot of time hanging out at my house.

I tried out for the basketball team and made it. I wasn't the best player, but I was fast and played good defense. TJ was team captain. I could tell he was really proud about it. Simon was team manager and he traveled with us to all of the games to keep score and manage the equipment.

Our team was having a really good season and we made it to the finals. And believe it or not, in our championship game, when the score was tied with only 20 seconds left on the clock, I sunk a 3 pointer to steal the victory.

When the ending buzzer rang, the crowd erupted in applause. TJ hoisted me on his shoulders and carried me off the court. "Let's hear it for Small Fry!" he shouted.

Things were really looking up. And the year was flying by. Ms. Riley kept us busy with all kinds of crazy projects, but she did have a way of making class interesting.

One day she brought a tadpole to school to show us how it "transforms". She had us sketch it in our notebooks so we could chart how it changes into a frog.

She called us to the back of the room to get a closer look at the tank. She pointed to the tadpole to show us where he was sprouting a leg. She went on and on about the "miraculous change."

We were busy sketching the tadpole and his "leg" in our Science journals, when Danielle raised her hand.

"Um. Ms. Riley. I don't actually think that's a leg," she said, eyeing the tadpole closely.

Ms. Riley looked confused and said, "It's got to be a leg, what else could it be?"

She pressed her nose against the glass and her eyebrows squished together. Some kids in the back started to giggle. I tried to keep a straight face because I was in the front row.

"Actually, I think it's excrement."

Ms. Riley's eyebrows shot up in surprise.

"Excre-what?" TJ shouted out. "Why don't you try speakin' English, Danielle."

She shot TJ a look and said, "Poop, I think it's poop. Is that clear enough for you, TJ?"

At that point the class lost it. I stared at the tadpole and the brown thing that was sprouting from its rear.

"Oh dear," Ms. Riley mumbled. "I think we better continue our study of the tadpoles another time."

Over the next few days a long brown string, which looked nothing like a leg, continued to sprout from the tadpole's body. Ms. Riley had us stop sketching his "miraculous change". But we secretly kept sketching the tadpole and his poop, taking bets on how long it would grow until it broke off. I know it's a little gross, but when you're in 6th grade you have to try to make things interesting. Wouldn't you know it, Danielle won.

Leave it to Danielle. She even knew everything about tadpole poop.

CHAPTER 22

Deadman's Curve

Things were going well and the year was flying by. During December, there was a day that was a really warm, which is unusual here in PA. The sun was shining, the sky was blue, and the snow had melted. Even the birds were confused, because they were sitting in the trees chirping, instead of flying South. I was outside with Simon shooting hoops, taking advantage of the nice weather, when Danielle and Emily rode up the street.

"Hey, do you guys want to go for a ride?" Emily asked, tossing her hair over her shoulder.

Emily was talking to me a lot lately. She smiled at me during class, the kind of smile she used to give Luke. Sometimes I had to turn around to make sure she wasn't looking at someone else, but sure enough it was me.

Danielle rolled her eyes and mumbled, "We're going to Deadman's Curve, if you want to come."

"Sure," I said, hopping on my bike.

It was kind of like old times, except now Emily was riding next to me and Danielle and Simon were following behind. I think they were having a good time back there. Danielle finally found someone she could boss around. Every once in a while, Emily would glance my way and smile and I'd have to try really hard not to lose my balance. Things seemed perfect.

"Those two are really hitting it off," I said, nodding toward Danielle and Simon. They were arguing about some kind of weird science thing.

We were riding along the narrow part of the trail that circles right above the river. It had rained a lot last week and the water was really roaring. I held my breath when I looked over the edge and saw the water rushing by in angry waves, but I tried to play it cool.

Emily giggled. "Yeah, they're quite a match." She glanced over her shoulder, but when she did her bike suddenly swerved to the side of the trail. I saw her heading for the edge and knew I had to act fast.

I sped up and raced to the side to push her back on track, but when I did I lost my balance. And that's when it happened.

My bike veered off the edge and suddenly I was barreling down the steep incline heading directly for the river. I plowed through sticks and brush. They were snapping and cracking and clawing my face and arms. I tried to brake, but it was no use. The hill was too steep. The raging water was moving fast in front of me. I saw a huge log lying on the riverbank. I thought that maybe if I hit it, I could stop. I aimed right for it. I crashed so hard that I flipped right over the handlebars and landed in the rushing water.

The icy river dragged me along. I tried to paddle to shore, but my right arm was numb and wouldn't move. The current pushed and shoved me and I tried to keep my head above the water, but it was getting harder. Just when I felt myself starting to sink, I was slammed into a branch in the middle of the river. I tried to crawl on top, but my leg wedged between the branch and a large rock that lay under the water. The current kept pulling me and I felt myself beginning to sink. I tried holding my breath, but I ended up gulping the water. Then everything went black.

CHAPTER 23

Hanging On

When I came to, Simon was above me trying to hold my head above the water. I guess when I fell, he jumped off his bike and slid down the hill. He ran down the river bank to where the big branch was and crawled out on his belly. Then he reached down and pulled my head above the water. He was kind of grabbing me by the hair and neck. I was coughing and sputtering, and I didn't really know what was happening.

Simon was shouting over the roaring water, "Hold on Alex. They're coming. The girls ran for help and someone should be here any minute."

I could tell he was really struggling because his face was sweaty and there was this big blue vein kind of pulsing on his forehead.

It felt like I was stuck there for an eternity with the freezing water numbing my skin. My head was pounding and things were looking fuzzy.

"Hold on, Alex," Simon whispered.

Then he got this weird look on his face and he started kind of huffing. I knew what was coming. He let out this huge sneeze that shook the branch. It cracked and started to break. We got real quiet and tried not to move at all, afraid that if we did the branch would snap and we'd be swept away.

Finally, we heard voices on the path above. The rescue crew rushed down the hill just in time. They threw a rope out to Simon which he tied around himself. He tried to loop it under my arms, but they were too far under the branch. He kept trying to reach down, but he couldn't quite get me. And every time he moved the branch would crack. He leaned over and ducked his head under the water. He had the rope around me and was starting to tie it, when the branch broke free and I felt myself being dragged with it. But Simon reached out and grabbed my hand. And he held on real tight as they pulled us to shore. The branch rushed down stream. We watched from the riverbank as it faded in the distance.

CHAPTER 24

Hometown Heroes

After the whole rescue at Deadman's curve, Simon and I were treated like big shots. I guess you could say I saved Emily, and Simon saved me. The paper even came and interviewed us. Our pictures were on the front page under the title: Hometown Heroes.

While I was in the hospital Emily sent me a card that thanked me for saving her. She cut the article out of the paper and put it in the card. At the bottom she drew a heart and inside she wrote *My Hero.*

I was in the hospital for a week. I had a concussion and broken arm which had to be set in three places. It sounds pretty bad, but the nurses took good care of me. And I finally had a room all to myself. But I did miss my family. They came to visit... a lot. And when they had to leave, Dylan would cling to me.

"I want Alex. I need my bwother to come home," he cried.

I smiled, "I promise, I'll be there soon."

When I finally came home, my parents had a special surprise waiting for me.

"Follow me, Alex," Mom said, as she guided me down the basement stairs. "Watch your step. We don't want any more injuries."

It took a minute for my eyes to adjust to the darkness. Then mom flipped a switch and the room lit up. I couldn't believe my eyes.

It was a bedroom- *my own bedroom!*

They had cornered of a section of the basement and put up a wall to divide it from dad's tool room. They had a throw rug on the floor and brought down all of my furniture. They even hung my basketball posters on the walls. It smelled a little musty, but it was worth it for some privacy.

"How do you like it?" Dad asked.

"It's awesome. Thank you," I replied.

"Well, we figured since you are growing up, it might be time to give you some space of your own," Dad said, patting me on the shoulder.

Mom smiled. "You're a great kid, Alex. And you're growing into a fine young man. In case we don't tell you enough, you make us very proud."

"Now, Mom, don't go getting all mushy on me." I said, hugging her with my good arm.

Dylan cried when he found out I wouldn't be staying with him, but I promised he could sleep over in my room on the weekends. He agreed.

Then he held out his bottle of monster spray and said, "Here, Alex. It's a little scawey down here. You can use this if you need it. My monstews are all gone now."

I smiled. "Thanks, Dude. You're a pretty cool little brother."

I returned to school before Christmas break, just in time for the talent show. And you'll never believe it, but I got up on that stage and sang *Born to Be Wild* in front of the whole school. And it wasn't

Karaoke. TJ played the guitar and we sounded pretty good. In fact, we won second prize in the show. But first prize went to someone who really deserved it. When the curtain opened to reveal Simon's painting, there was no doubt that he should win. The man in the painting had dark hair and kind eyes framed by thick glasses. He looked a whole lot like Simon, but older.

I knew who it was right away.

And when Simon climbed the steps to the stage wearing his saddle shoes, I knew that man would be proud of him.

Our class celebrated with a Burger Boat party. My dad, who had been recently promoted to manager, donated captain meals for my entire class. Everyone loved his pirate suit and they all said I was so lucky that my Dad worked there.

Yeah, I was pretty lucky. It just took me a while to realize it.

Luke returned home during that Christmas break. When he saw me, he smiled and said, "You seem different, Dude. Did you grow or something?"

I nodded and said, "Yeah." I had grown, in more ways than one.

Thanks to my family for their love, support, and patience.

Thanks to my writing group for helping me develop this story.

Made in the USA
Monee, IL
13 May 2022